STANLEY

Based on *The Railway Series* by the Rev. W. Awdry

Illustrations by
Robin Davies

EGMONT

EGMONT

We bring stories to life

First published in Great Britain in 2009
by Egmont UK Limited
239 Kensington High Street, London W8 6SA

Thomas the Tank Engine & Friends™

CREATED BY BRITT ALLCROFT

HiT entertainment

ISBN 978 1 4052 4423 7
1 3 5 7 9 10 8 6 4 2
Printed in Italy

FSC
Mixed Sources
Product group from well-managed
forests and other controlled sources
Cert no. TT-COC-002332
www.fsc.org
© 1996 Forest Stewardship Council

*T*his is a story about Stanley, a powerful engine with a shiny silver funnel. Thomas wanted to be the 'leader of the tracks' but Stanley showed him that Really Useful Engines work together …

One day, when Thomas was exploring, he found the lost town of Great Waterton.

The Fat Controller was very pleased. He put Thomas in charge of rebuilding the town before the Sodor Day celebrations.

"I'm the leader of the tracks!" sang Thomas.

Just then, Gordon raced past with a new grey and red engine. He was bigger than Thomas.

"I wonder who he is?" Thomas thought.

When Thomas reached the Sheds, he saw that the new engine was already there.

"This is Stanley," said The Fat Controller. "He will do Thomas' work while Thomas takes charge at Great Waterton."

Stanley blew a puff of steam and smiled.

"Stanley looks strong and fast," Gordon told Thomas. "He'll be a Really Useful Engine."

But Thomas was too excited about his important new job to worry about Stanley taking his place.

The next day, when Thomas went past the wash down, he saw a funny sight. Percy and Stanley were covered in bubbles!

"Hello!" tooted Thomas. "That looks like fun!"

But Percy and Stanley were chuckling so much that they didn't even notice Thomas.

Thomas felt cross. He wanted to show everyone that he was the most Useful Engine on Sodor.

So later that day, he raced along pulling some heavy trucks, to show how strong and fast he was.

Then there was trouble. Thomas took a corner too quickly and slipped off the track!

The Fat Controller was cross. "Thomas, you must go to the Works to be mended!" he shouted. "Stanley can take your place at Great Waterton."

Once Thomas had been repaired, he sped back to Great Waterton.

The Fat Controller said, "Stanley's done well. He'll stay in charge. You can help him, Thomas."

Poor Thomas! He had lost his important job and now Stanley had taken his place!

Then Thomas had a naughty idea.

"If I shunt lots of trucks, Stanley won't be able to pull them all. Then everyone will see he's not so Useful and I'll be in charge again!"

Poor Stanley huffed and puffed, pulling all the trucks up the hill. He wasn't going to give up!

Suddenly, a coupling snapped and the trucks rolled back down the hill. BANG! They crashed into Waterton Tower, knocking it down!

"Disaster!" roared The Fat Controller. "Thomas, why did you shunt so many trucks for Stanley?"

Thomas felt so ashamed. He couldn't tell The Fat Controller why he had done it.

That night, when everyone was asleep, Thomas decided to make up for his naughty trick.

He worked all night, shunting trucks. By the morning, nearly all the work was done.

One truck had been left behind, in front of a mineshaft. "I'll fix that!" said Thomas. But he biffed the truck too hard and it trundled into the mine.

Thomas puffed down the dark tunnel to fetch the truck. But the track was flooded! His wheels slipped and he slid into the darkness.

Back in Great Waterton, Stanley asked the engines if they had seen Thomas. No one had.

"He looked very sorry when the trucks crashed," said Stanley. "I'm sure he didn't do it on purpose."

The Fat Controller was worried. "Everyone must look for Thomas!" he boomed.

Stanley knew how important Thomas was.

"I'll find Thomas and tell him we all miss him," he said to himself.

Meanwhile, Thomas was sliding along the flooded mine tracks. Then all of a sudden, the tunnel opened out on to the hillside.

"Bust my buffers!" wheeshed Thomas, as he sped down the hill.

He came to a stop beside an old track. Poor Thomas could only wait and whistle for help.

"I *am* silly," he said. "Stanley wasn't trying to take my place. He was just trying to be Useful, like me."

Stanley searched the hills but he couldn't find Thomas. It was time to go back to Waterton. He blew his whistle once more, as loudly as he could.

Thomas heard him and whistled back!

"Thomas!" Stanley said, as he chugged towards him. "Where have you been? Did you run away?"

"No. I was just trying to be Useful," said Thomas, and he told Stanley all about his adventure.

"Sorry I played a trick on you, Stanley," peeped Thomas, as Stanley heaved him up on to the rails.

"Let's be friends," Stanley huffed.

Then came a loud CRACK! Stanley had burst a valve in his boiler. Now *he* couldn't move!

"Don't worry," whistled Thomas. "It's my turn to help you!"

So, puff by puff, Thomas helped Stanley back to Great Waterton.

Everyone worked hard to rebuild the Tower and finished just in time . . . Sodor Day had arrived!

"Thomas, I want you to bring the Mayor to the special celebrations," said The Fat Controller.

"Please, Sir," tooted Thomas, "can Stanley do it?"

"You can do it together," he replied. "After all, Stanley saved you and you saved Stanley."

So Stanley puffed proudly into Great Waterton with the Mayor on board and his new friend, Thomas, by his side!

TWO Great Offers for Thomas Fans!

In every Thomas Story Library book like this one, you will find a special token. Collect the tokens and claim exclusive Thomas goodies:

Offer 1

Collect 6 tokens and we'll send you a **poster** and a **bookmark** for only **£1.** (to cover P&P)

My Thomas Story Library - Collect them all

Thomas books available to buy online at www.egmont.co.uk

Available to buy online at www.egmont.co.uk
Look out for 5 NEW Thomas Story Library books in August 2009!

Reply Card for Thomas Goodies!

1 Yes, please send me a **Thomas poster and bookmark.**
I have enclosed **6 tokens plus a £1 coin** to cover P&P. ☐

2 Yes, please send me a **Thomas book bag.**
I have enclosed **12 tokens plus £2** to cover P&P. ☐

Simply fill in your details below and send them to:
Thomas Offers, PO BOX 715, Horsham, RH12 5WG

Fan's Name: ....

Address: ....

....

.... Date of Birth: ....

Email: ....

Name of parent/guardian: ....

Signature of parent/guardian: ....

Please allow 28 days for delivery. Offer is only available while stocks last. We reserve the right
to change the terms of this offer at any time and we offer a 14 day money back guarantee.
This does not affect your statutory rights. Offer applies to UK only. The cost applies to Postage
and Packaging (P&P).

We may occasionally wish to send you information about other Egmont children's books but if
you would rather we didn't please tick here ☐